BL-2.8
P-0.5

# A Dog's Best Friend

**MASSIMO
MOSTACCHI**

**MONICA
MICELI**

# A Dog's Best Friend

A MICHAEL NEUGEBAUER BOOK / NORTH-SOUTH BOOKS / NEW YORK / LONDON

There really was no reason for Dudley to be sad.
He had the kindest master in town.
He had the softest bed and the best food.
But something was missing in his life, and Dudley
decided to go out and find it.

So early one morning before his master was awake,
Dudley crept out of the house and through the town,
and ran far out into the country.

That night he slept in a field, and when he woke up he saw
a group of animals under a tree.

As he crept closer, he saw that it was a bunch of nice, fat pigs.

"Hello!" said the fattest pig of all. "What can we do for you today?"

"I . . . I don't know," stuttered Dudley. "I . . . I've run away from home."

"Then you must stay with us. We have a great time here. We eat big meals, we roll in the mud when it's hot, and we sleep all we want. It's a wonderful life!"

So Dudley stayed, and soon he began to look like a pig. His paws grew into hooves and his tail curled. And instead of barking, he grunted.

One day the farmer came to choose the fattest pigs
to take to market.
Dudley was the first one to be put on the truck.

At the market the other animals looked at Dudley.
They whispered to each other.
The goose hissed, "Is that thing supposed to be a pig?"
And the sheep said, "Just baa-baarely! More like a pig-dog
if you ask me-e-e-ee!"
All the other animals laughed.
Feeling ashamed, Dudley tucked his curly tail between
his legs and ran away.

He ran most of the night, until he came to a barn.
"Who-haw are you-haw?" said a voice from the darkness.
It was a donkey standing by the window.
"Now I see-haw," said the donkey. "You-haw are a dog—hee-haw!"
Dudley could see it was true. He no longer looked like a pig.
So Dudley told the donkey about his troubles.
"I see-haw!" said the donkey. "You-haw should stay-haw with
me-haw!"

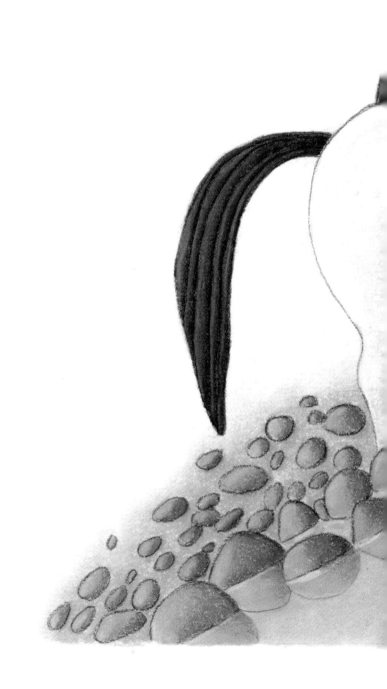

So Dudley stayed.
And soon he began to look like a donkey.
His ears got long, and his tail got long.
And instead of barking, he brayed.

One day the owners came to pack heavy loads onto the donkeys, and Dudley got the heaviest load of all.
Up and up the steep mountain path they went, until Dudley was too tired to go on.
"Psst!" said a rabbit. "Psst! Come with me! You're not a donkey!"
"I know-haw!" said Dudley, and he ran off after the rabbit.

Who would have thought that rabbits could be so friendly? Dudley tossed off his heavy load, and ran and tumbled with the rabbit and all his friends. That night as he curled up to sleep beneath a bush, he thought, "I could enjoy being a rabbit!"

And in the morning, that's just what he looked like.
So he stayed with the rabbits, and each day
was more fun than the last one.

Then one day, BOOM! BANG! BOOM! Hunters!
Dudley was terrified, and ran off as fast and as far
as his rabbit-dog legs would carry him.

Dudley finally sat down on a hilltop with his own doggy tongue hanging out, and right there below him was his very own town and his very own house.

Dudley ran through the streets until he came to his
house. There, in his very own window, was—another dog!
"What are you doing here?" growled Dudley.
"I live here," said the other dog. "What are you doing here?"
"I live here too!" said Dudley.
And the new dog said, "You do? Great! I've been here for weeks
with no one to play with. I was so sad, I was going to run away.
But this changes everything!"

From that day on, Dudley and Tuck were just a couple of dogs. They were best friends, and they were happy. And life doesn't get much better than that.

English adaptation by Andrew Clements

Copyright © 1995 by Michael Neugebauer Verlag AG, Gossau Zürich, Switzerland.
First published in Switzerland under the title *Kopf hoch, Dodi!*
English translation copyright © 1995 by North-South Books Inc.

First published in the United States, Canada, Great Britain, Australia, and New Zealand in 1995
by North-South Books, an imprint of Nord-Süd Verlag AG, Gossau Zürich, Switzerland.

Distributed in the United States by North-South Books Inc., New York.

Library of Congress Cataloging-in-Publication Data is available.
A CIP catalogue record for this book is available from The British Library.
ISBN 1-55858-497-8 (trade binding) 10 9 8 7 6 5 4 3 2 1
ISBN 1-55858-498-6 (library binding) 10 9 8 7 6 5 4 3 2 1
Printed in Belgium